Mr. Bear's Picnic

Debi Gliori

ARTISTS & WRITERS GUILD BOOKS
Golden Books
Western Publishing Company, Inc.

with grateful thanks for
the thousand small kindnesses
shown to me by
everyone working on Ward 49
of Simpson's Maternity Pavilion
through the summer of 1994

This book is dedicated to
all of you with my love.

First published in Great Britain in 1995 by Orchard Books.

Library of Congress Cataloging–in–Publication Data:
Gliori, Debi.
Mr. Bear's picnic / by Debi Gliori.
p.   cm.
"Artists & Writers Guild books."
Summary: Mr. Bear plans to take the baby out for the day, but when the three
Grizzly-Bear cubs tab along, everyone is in for some surprises.
[1. Bears--Fiction. 2. Picnicking--Fiction.] I. Title.
PZ7.G4889Mt 1995   [E]--dc20   94-31363   CIP   AC

"What a beautiful day!" said Mr. Bear
as soon as he opened his eyes. He crept
out of bed, trying not to wake Mrs. Bear.

"It's perfect for a picnic," he said softly.
"I think I'll take the baby out for the day."

Mrs. Bear opened one bleary eye.
"Mmm, that's a good idea," she yawned.
Then she turned over and went back to sleep.

As Mr. Bear and the baby walked past the
Grizzly-Bears' house, they heard voices from
the branches above them.

"Here we are, Mr. Bear," said Fred.
"Are you going on a picnic?" said Ted.
"Can we come, too?" said Fuzz.
Mr. Bear groaned.
"Please?" begged Fred, Ted, and Fuzz. And they tumbled out of the tree in a furry heap and ran to tell Mrs. Grizzly-Bear where they were going.

It took a long time to choose
a good place for the picnic.

Mr. Bear thought the
first spot was just right.
"Dad *always* brings us here,"
moaned Fred. "It's *boring*."

Mr. Bear thought the
next spot was interesting.
"This is a fly-infested
swamp," said Ted.

Everyone agreed that the third
spot was too quiet and gloomy.
"This place gives me the creeps,"
said Fuzz.

At last Mr. Bear found the perfect place. He put his baby down in a grassy hollow and the picnic basket under a tree. He was just stretching out in the sun for a little snooze when Fred bounced onto his stomach.

"I'm starving," said Fred. "I could eat six sandwiches."

"I'm ravenous," said Ted. "I could eat six sandwiches and whatever else is in that basket."

"I'm famished," said Fuzz. "I could eat six sandwiches, whatever else is in that basket, and the basket as well."

Mr. Bear left his comfortable
spot with a sigh. "Okay. We'll have
something to eat. Let's see what we've
got for lunch." He opened the picnic basket.
Inside was a teddy bear, a set of blocks,
and some toys with wheels.

"You can't eat toys," said Fred, glaring at Mr. Bear.
"I think you brought the wrong basket," said Ted.
"What are we going to eat?" said Fuzz.
The baby began to cry.

"I know," said Mr. Bear. "We'll have fish for
our picnic." And he strode off to a rock where
he balanced his baby on his shoulders, dipped
a paw in the water, and waited.

"What's taking so long?" asked Fred while Ted
and Fuzz watched.

"Maybe I should wiggle my paw like a worm,"
said Mr. Bear. "I know I could catch something
if I just . . . s-t-r-e-t-c-h-e-d . . . a bit . . . farther."

"HHLLBBBBLUB" said Mr Bear,
slipping headfirst into the pond.
"Dablublublub," cried his baby,
clinging tightly to his ear.

"You're not supposed to fall in," said Fred.
"Our Dad never gets wet when he goes fishing,"
said Ted. "And he always catches lots of fish."
"All you're going to catch is a cold," added Fuzz.
"I don't think we're going to have a picnic, after all."

"Oh, yes, we are!" declared Mr. Bear.
"Shhh, you'll scare away the fish," said Fred.
"You know, I don't even like fish," said Ted.

"WHAAAAT?" said Mr. Bear.
"Dad makes us eat loads of fish," said Fuzz.
". . . with all the jaggedy bones," added Fred.
". . . and the slimy skin," said Ted.
". . . and the yucky eyeballs," said Fuzz.
"Well, never mind the fish," said Mr. Bear. "Follow me. I know just what you bears need to eat."

The young Grizzly-Bears trailed up the hill
behind Mr. Bear. They were all getting tired.
"Look!" he told them. "It's just a little bit farther."
Overhead, tucked in the branches of a tree, was
a golden dome. Mr. Bear put the basket down,
settled his baby in it, and climbed the tree.

Fred, Ted, and Fuzz watched in
amazement as Mr. Bear gently dipped
his paw into the golden dome surrounded
by buzzing bees.

"You're really good at that," said Fred.

"When our Dad does that, he gets stung,"
said Ted.

"And then he falls," said Fuzz.

Mr. Bear pulled out a big chunk of
honeycomb. He climbed out of the tree
and gave everyone a taste of the honey.
"I love honey," said Fred.

"I could eat the whole honeycomb and
the hive it came from," said Ted.
"I could eat the whole honeycomb,
the hive, and the bees as well," said Fuzz.
And they all started for home.

When they got there, Mrs. Bear
and the Grizzly-Bears were waiting
for them.

"You took the wrong picnic basket,"
said Mrs. Bear. "All of you must be
starving."

"No," said Fred. "We found
lots of honey."

"You should see Mr. Bear
gathering honey," said Ted.
"He's really good at it!"

"And we saved some for
you," said Fuzz.

Mr. Bear smiled from ear to ear.
"Bread and honey for dinner," he said.
And they all sat down and had a tasty feast.